KT-222-716

The Biggest Kiss

To Ivo – *JW*

To my biggest beloved
kisser, Luca – *JA*

SIMON AND SCHUSTER
First published in Great Britain in 2010 by Simon and Schuster UK Ltd
1st Floor, 222 Gray's Inn Road, London WC1X 8HB
A CBS Company

Text copyright © 2010 Joanna Walsh
Illustrations copyright © 2010 Giuditta Gaviraghi

The right of Joanna Walsh and Giuditta Gaviraghi to be identified as the author and illustrator of
this work has been asserted by them in accordance with the Copyright, Designs and Patents Act, 1988
All rights reserved, including the right of reproduction in whole or in part in any form
A CIP catalogue record for this book is available from the British Library upon request

ISBN: 978-1-84738-435-5 (HB)
ISBN: 978-1-84738-436-2 (PB)
Printed in Italy
2 4 6 8 10 9 7 5 3

The Biggest Kiss

Joanna Walsh & Judi Abbot

SIMON AND SCHUSTER
London New York Sydney

Kisses on noses,

kisses on toes-es.

Sudden **kisses** when you least supposes.

Who likes to **kiss**?

I do! I do! Even the shy do.

Why not try, too?

Frogs like to **kiss**,

and dogs like to **kiss.**

'normous
elephants do.

Little tiny ants do.

Do worms **kiss** underground, with the soil all around?

Do fish **kiss**
like this —

splosh,

splash,

splish?

Some **kisses** are misses,
they land on the ear or near.
But **kisses** with lipstick stick like . . .

a **kiss** with honey,

a **kiss** that's yummy,

a **kiss** on the elbow,

a **kiss** on the tummy.

The rain's **kiss** on your skin is fun.

The snow's **kiss** on your face is ace.

The
TALLEST
kiss is a
tricky kind.

The smallest kiss is hard to find.

Bye-bye
kisses,

fly-high
kisses,

eye-dry
kisses,

all my
kisses.

I wish for a **kiss** before breakfast,
to start the day right.

And a **kiss** at the end
to say, "Good night!"

I've had all these **kisses**,
and lots more too.

But the very
best kiss . . .

is a **kiss** from you!